Be Good to Eddie Lee

Virginia Fleming

ILLUSTRATED BY
Floyd Cooper

Philomel Books
NEW YORK

Text copyright © 1993 by Virginia Fleming
Illustrations copyright © 1993 by Floyd Cooper
Published by Philomel Books, a division of the Putnam & Grosset
Group, 200 Madison Avenue, New York, NY 10016.
All rights reserved. This book, or parts thereof, may not be reproduced
in any form without permission in writing from the publisher.
Published simultaneously in Canada.
Printed in Hong Kong by South China Printing Co. (1988) Ltd.
The text is set in Palatino. Lettering by David Gatti.

The artist used an oil wash on board to create the illustrations
for this book.

Library of Congress Cataloging-in-Publication Data
Fleming, Virginia. Be good to Eddie Lee / by Virginia Fleming;
illustrated by Floyd Cooper. p. cm.
Summary: Although Christy considered him a pest, when Eddie Lee,
a boy with Down's syndrome, follows her into the woods,
he shares several special discoveries with her.
[1. Down's syndrome—Fiction. 2. Mentally handicapped—Fiction.]
I. Cooper, Floyd, ill. II. Title. PZ7.F626Be   1993
91-46146 CIP AC [E]—dc20
ISBN 0-399-21993-5

3 5 7 9 10 8 6 4 2

To Gary, my special friend,
and for Zachary, Ryan, Eric, and Joshua

—V. F.

For Velma

—F. C.

Christy glided back and forth in the porch swing, letting her legs dangle. Now that summer was here, she didn't know what to do with it. She grabbed a leaf from a trumpet vine. Across the street, Eddie Lee was sitting on his front-porch steps eating a popsicle.

"Now I'll be bothered with him following me around all summer," she thought.

Her mama said she had to be good to Eddie Lee. Just because he was lonesome. Just because nobody else paid him any mind. Just because he was different.

Her mama said God made him that way. But Christy thought maybe, just once, her mama was wrong, because God didn't make mistakes, and Eddie Lee was a mistake if there ever was one.

In the next yard up she could see JimBud. He was tossing marbles, trying to get them in a hole. She left the swing and walked slowly up the street, pretending not to notice him.

"Hello, Christy."

She climbed up on his fence and scuffed her sneakers into the bottom board.

"Hello, JimBud," she said. JimBud tossed his last marble into the hole and climbed up beside her.

"Phew, it's hot," he said. He took off his sneakers. "Warm enough to go wadin'. Want to go with me? I know where there's frog eggs."

Christy nodded and they hid their shoes under the pyracantha bush and started down the street.

As they passed Eddie Lee's house, he called eagerly, "Hello, Christy! Hello, JimBud!"

JimBud tugged at her arm. "Come on. Don't stop to talk to that dummy."

Eddie Lee waddled down the steps and out into the street, chocolate running down his chin onto his shirt. He wore a big grin. JimBud ignored him, so Christy said, "Eddie Lee, you'd better stay home."

He didn't say anything, just looked hurt. Christy wished she had brought him an all-day sucker or something.

JimBud gave her another tug. "Come on, Christy!"

"Eddie Lee, I said GO HOME. G–O H–O–M–E!"

"Ah, creeps, Christy, he can't spell."

JimBud whirled around and stamped his foot. "GET, Eddie Lee! Get home!"

Eddie Lee grinned. "I'm not a dog, JimBud."

"Then stop followin' us like one."

Eddie Lee turned around and walked toward his house, head down.

"You didn't have to hurt his feelings, JimBud. Mama says I have to be good to Eddie Lee."

They had to go through the woods to reach the lake. Christy liked the smell of the wet leaves and the tickle of the soft ferns on her bare legs. The ground felt hard and cold to her feet.

"What's that?" Christy asked.

There was an ear-tingling rattle as a belted kingfisher left its perch and flew like a silver streak out over the lake. It hovered above the lake for seconds, then, after diving into the water, surfaced with a crayfish in its beak.

JimBud dipped his toes into the water, testing it. "There goes a fish!" he yelled.

"I don't see any frog eggs," Christy said.
"They have probably already hatched."
He most likely made it up about the frog eggs, just so she would come with him. Christy let her feet sink into the bottom sand and it curled about her toes like the folds of her downy quilt.

Suddenly a strange, shuffling sound came from the bushes near the trail.

"What was that?" JimBud looked scared.

"I dunno."

They moved closer to one another and listened. THUMP! THUMP! Christy's heart began to pound. They looked around for a place to run. The tall reeds around the edge of the lake made a quick escape impossible.

"Sounds like a monster," JimBud whispered.

The bushes parted and the "monster" came clopping down the trail. It was Eddie Lee.

"What are *you* doin' here?" JimBud screamed. He looked at Christy and told a whopper. "I knew it was him, all the time." But there was a squeaky little quiver in his voice and Christy knew that he had been just as frightened as she was. Eddie Lee just sat down on the bank and looked at them.

"Look, JimBud, there's a salamander! A teeny-weeny baby." Christy pointed to the tiny animal squirming at the edge of the lake. JimBud squatted down beside her. Suddenly there was a great splash.

"I got him, JimBud!" Eddie Lee crooned. He scooped up the tiny salamander in his hands.

"Now look what you did, Eddie Lee!" JimBud shouted, looking down at his soaked jeans. "Just leave us alone."

Eddie Lee turned to Christy. "Here, Christy, you can have it."

She held out her hands, and felt the gentleness as he carefully let the salamander slip from his hands into hers.

"I still don't see any frog eggs," Christy complained as they waded along the edge of the lake again.

"BEE–U–TI–FUL!" Behind them, Eddie Lee stood looking out over the lake with his arms outstretched, his almond eyes charmed by water lilies that spread across the water's surface like a patchwork quilt. "BEE–U–TI–FUL!"

Christy looked up and, for the first time, saw the lilies.

"Oh, they are beautiful! JimBud, do you suppose we could pick some for Mama? Even one. She could put it in a glass bowl in the center of the table."

"They're way out in the lake!" JimBud said.

"I'll get you a lily, Christy," Eddie Lee said. He splish-splashed through the water until it reached his knees, but the lilies were far beyond his reach. Disappointed, he waded back, his shoes squeaky wet.

"I told you he was a dummy," JimBud said.

Eddie Lee turned away from them and ran into the woods.

"Now see what you've done? You've hurt his feelings."

JimBud shrugged and started off toward the cove side of the lake. Christy followed.

They had hardly reached it when THUMP! THUMP! This time they were not frightened. They knew it was Eddie Lee. THUMP! THUMP! SQUISH! SQUISH! His face was red. He had been running.

"Come on, Christy!" Eddie Lee took her hand and pulled.

"Where?"

"Come on, I'll show you."

She left JimBud sitting on the bank and followed Eddie Lee, who was now waddling into the woods.

"Come on," he called. "I'll show you." He led her along a trail that followed the edge of the lake, past beaver-gnawed birches, over roots and across a gravelly stream. Suddenly he rushed ahead.

"Here it is." He smiled proudly.

There was a wide opening in the trail, and right there, in the woods, was a miniature lake. Tall grass surrounded the edge. A swamp sparrow trilled from an overhanging branch. The pond lay clear and shadowy in the cool of the June afternoon. Floating on the surface of the pond were myriad pink and white lilies. In all the times Christy had come to the woods, she had never seen this pond.

She knelt down and leaned over to look into the water. She could see her reflection in the pool. She was wearing a crown of lilies. Eddie Lee's reflection smiled at her.

But he still wanted something.

"Come on, Christy, I'll show you." He reached for her hand and pulled her with him as he trailed around the little pond to the far end.

"Look!" he shouted, pointing to the still, sun-warmed water. There, clusters of frog eggs were settled on the bottom mud, large cloudlike jelly masses, polka-dotted with tiny tadpoles not ready to hatch.

"Frog eggs! Oh, Eddie Lee, you are a genius! You found water lilies *and* frog eggs!" She bent down and touched the soft, silky mass. The sun shone on patches of it. Some of the tadpoles were moving.

"We have to find something to put them in," Christy said.

Eddie Lee's almond eyes slid together and his forehead folded to a frown. "No! No!" he said.

"Yes, so we can take them home in a jar or something."

Eddie Lee pointed his finger at her. His words came out slowly, as if he had to think about them first. "If we take them home, they will die. The mama frog…Christy…the mama frog…" He couldn't get the rest out.

"Will be sad," Christy finished. "I never thought of that. Well, Eddie Lee, let's go pick a lily for Mama anyway."

Just as they got down on their knees to reach for the lilies, there was a *plop* in the water. The water rippled into circles, one inside another. Eddie Lee pointed to their reflections and laughed.

"You look funny, Christy."

Christy's face in the water-mirror was distorted by the ripples. She put her hands to her cheeks to hide the crooked image.

"That's okay, Christy," he said. "I like you, anyway."
He grinned his wide grin and put his right hand over
his heart. "It's what's here that counts."

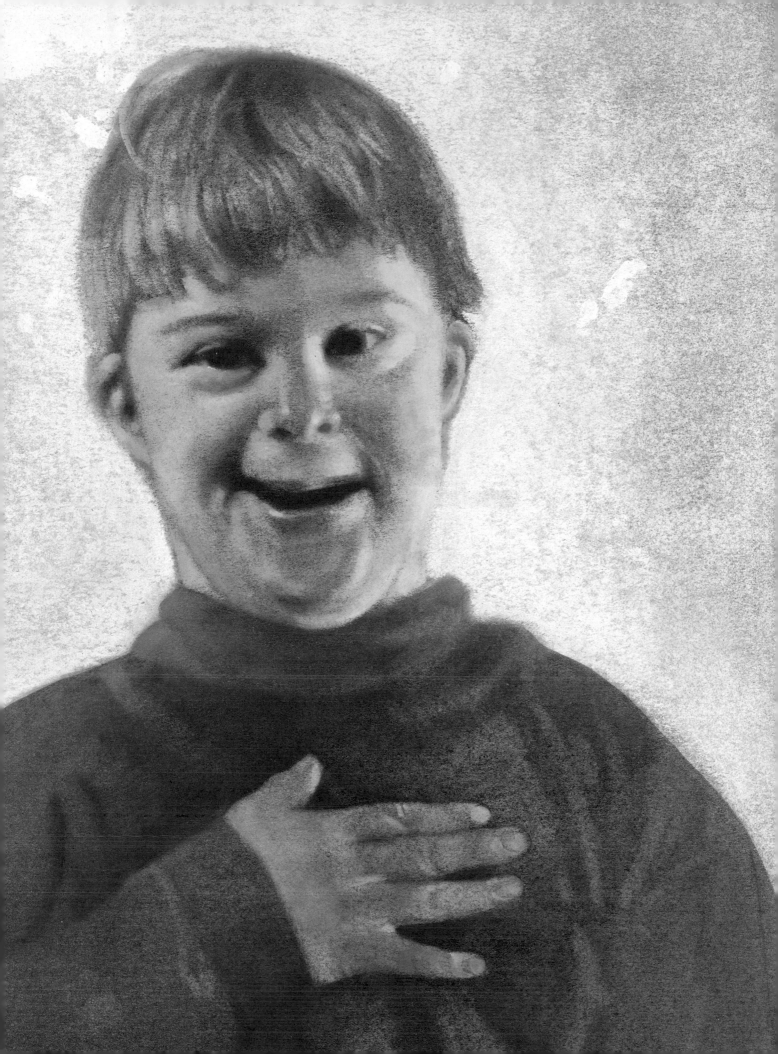

The two started back through the woods. "JimBud!" Christy called.
The path was filled with afternoon sun. "Wait till you see!"